HOT RESPONSE

City General: Medic 1 Series

Book 1

RUBY SCOTT

D&V

Ruby Scott

Bought From Me?
Let Me Sign Your Ebook

If you bought ebooks direct from me, you can get these signed with a personal message written just for you, along with one of my sapphic doodles.

Head over to my webshop to order a signed ebook

Independent authors like me are completely dependent on reviews. The truth is simple:

Good reviews = Amazon recommending this book = my ability to write more stories.

You don't even need to write words—just leaving a quick ★★★★★ rating is enough to make a huge difference.

☞ **Leave your review here:**
1. **AMAZON REVIEWS**
2. **<u>APPLE REVIEWS</u>**
2. **GOODREADS REVIEWS**
3. **RUBYSCOTT.SHOP REVIEWS**

Thank you from Chrissie, Sam and Ruby!

———————————————————

A Thought...

———————————————————

"But the worst enemy you can meet will always be yourself;
you lie in wait for yourself in caverns and forest."

- Friedrich Nietzsche, Thus Spoke Zarathustra

Chapter 1

"Mom? Mom, can you hear me? Mom, please. Mom!"

Sam jerked awake with a strangled cry, her hands reaching out for the ghost of a woman who wasn't there—a woman who hadn't been there for years. For a few seconds, she struggled to breathe, just like she always did when she woke from a nightmare about the crash, and then she remembered where she was.

It was five years on. She was in bed, in her apartment, and it was dark because it was three a.m., not because she was upside down on a snowy embankment. That pain across her chest where the seatbelt was cutting into her skin wasn't real, and the harsh smell of gasoline that burned her nose was just a phantom.

She sank back against the pillows shakily, counting down from ten. It was a tactic her therapist had taught her in the months after the accident. Sometimes it worked, sometimes it didn't, but it was always worth a try.

"Ten."

She was at home, in bed…

"Nine."

The desperation in her voice as she cried out for her mother was fading now, getting quieter…

"Eight."

Her voice was growing stronger; it had lost that shaky quality that betrayed her nerves.

"Seven. Six."

Her breathing was steadier now.

"Five."

The smell of gasoline got weaker, replaced by the lavender diffuser in the corner of her room. She kept counting, all the way down to one, and when she was finished, she felt her muscles relax a little. For a few moments, she lay in the darkness staring at the ceiling before allowing exhaustion to take over, dragging her into a dreamless sleep for the few remaining hours before her alarm was set to awaken her.

As she waited for her first coffee of the morning to brew, Sam leaned against the kitchen counter, staring off into space as she thought about the nightmare that had woken her the night before.

It wasn't often she had nightmares anymore. The year after the crash had been the worst—she'd woken up almost every night screaming for her mother until her throat was raw, desperately scrabbling at the air in front of her as she tried to cling onto a woman who was long gone. But after a while it got a little easier to deal with the loss. It always did, in the end. The pain got just a little less agonizing; the grief was just a little less overwhelming, and the nightmares grew more infrequent.

As she poured her coffee, Sam wondered what had set her

off, before remembering the patient she'd dealt with the day before. She was a young girl, couldn't have been much older than eighteen, and she'd lost control of her car as she made her way home. She'd taken a turn too quickly, flown off the road, and wrapped herself around a lamppost.

The car was a mangled wreck when they'd arrived, but she was alive. Sam couldn't help but wince as she remembered the terror in the young girl's face when she'd looked up at the EMTs. She wondered if that was how she'd looked all those years ago. Young, terrified, not sure if she was dead or alive.

That familiar sick feeling swirled in her stomach, but Sam pushed it down as she sipped her coffee, huffing out a breath through her nose. The girl was okay, except for the broken bones and bruises. That was what mattered, that was what she had to focus on.

With a low groan, Sam stretched out her aching muscles slowly. At least she didn't have to work today. There was no risk of accidentally stumbling on a job that would trigger another nightmare. All she had was soccer practice in a few hours.

Sam had found the soccer team a couple of years earlier, on the recommendation of her therapist. Sports were a regularly recommended form of therapy for people who'd gone through trauma. Team sports forced you to interact with people and reduce the risk of isolating yourself and falling into depression, or something like that. Honestly, Sam had just taken it up because it gave her the excuse to kick something, and back then that was all she'd wanted.

It had quickly become so much more than that, though. Maybe it was the fact that she was naturally good at soccer, or maybe she really did just like team sports, but Sam had grown to genuinely love the sport. She loved the feeling of chasing down the field, loved the adrenaline that pulsed through her veins the moment the game started, and she'd fallen in love with her teammates almost instantly.

In fact, practice probably would have been perfect if not for one tiny detail—her hardass coach, Chrissie. For some reason, the older woman had taken an instant dislike to Sam from the first day she joined the team, and after months of quiet comments and pointed jabs, she was making no effort at hiding it.

It might not have been so bad if it wasn't for the fact that Chrissie wasn't just technically her boss on the field. When Sam had started her probation as an EMT a month earlier, she'd been told she would work alongside one of the most experienced members of the team. Her new partner was someone who took rookies under her wing all the time, so there was nothing to worry about.

She'd been horrified to walk into the break room and see Chrissie waiting for her. Not only did she have to put up with *Coach* Chrissie snapping at her when she was late to practice, or made a little mistake during a game, but now she had to contend with *EMT* Chrissie too.

Sam shuddered dramatically at the thought, sipping her coffee. She'd thought Coach Chrissie was bad, but EMT Chrissie played in a totally different league. It was understandable—they were holding people's lives in their hands every day—but even so, it rubbed her the wrong way.

She let out a long, languid sigh as she threw herself down on the couch. At least she didn't have work today. That meant she only had to see that disappointed look on Chrissie's face for a couple of hours at practice that afternoon. Until then, she could freely binge-watch another season of *Scrubs* on the TV.

Chapter 2

It was ten past the hour, which meant it had been fifteen minutes since Chrissie had expected the team on the soccer field. She'd counted them off one by one as they'd strolled out of the changing rooms, and she was one short.

She didn't even need to scour the faces of the ten women in front of her to know which one was missing from the lineup.

"Let me guess." She heard a familiar voice beside her, and turned on the spot to see Terri, the goalkeeper of the team. She'd popped up beside Chrissie, rather than warming up with the rest of the team. "O'Shea again?"

Chrissie just grunted in response, digging around in the pocket of her windbreaker for her chewing gum. "Always is, isn't it?"

Terri just laughed, twisting from side to side in a lazy attempt at a warmup. "At least she's consistent."

"I'd prefer it if she was consistently *here*," Chrissie muttered, more to herself than to Terri. "And don't forget to stretch out your hamstrings."

Terri breathed out a sigh, feigning annoyance. "Damn,

coach. It's almost like I've been playing soccer since sixth grade."

A hint of a smile threatened to soften the frown on Chrissie's face as a familiar silver car pulled up in the parking lot by the field. Terri was an old friend from work she'd corralled into playing for her team years earlier, so there was always a little hint of sarcasm whenever she called Chrissie 'coach'. Chrissie wouldn't have allowed it from anyone else, but she figured Terri had earned it after all the time they'd spent cramped up together in the back of ambulances.

"Oh, look who showed up." Terri had spotted the car too. The driver's door opened and out stepped Sam O'Shea, already dressed in her kit (thankfully). She nudged her door shut with a bump of her hip, and jogged towards the field, struggling to tie her long blonde hair back into a loose ponytail as she did.

She must have sensed the oncoming lecture that was gearing up in Chrissie's head because she was rattling off an apology before she even reached them. Her cheeks were flushed a light rose from the cold autumnal air, and as she approached Chrissie and Terri, they could see little wisps of blonde hair already coming astray from the ponytail.

"You're late, O'Shea," Chrissie said coldly, cutting across the apology without listening to whatever excuse she'd come up with today.

Once she was on the field, Sam was one of the best players on the team. For someone who came across so bright and bubbly in her day to day life, she had a fearsome competitive streak during a game that Chrissie appreciated. It was getting her onto the field that always proved to be a problem. She was always the last on the field, whether she was taking her time in the locker room or arriving late.

"Hurry up and warm up with the others," Chrissie continued, waving her over towards the rest of the team with a dismissive flick of her wrist. The rest of the apology died on Sam's lips, and Chrissie saw something flash across her features—anger, annoyance or frustration, she wasn't sure which. "Get moving before I change my mind and make you do laps."

There was a beat of silence that followed the order, punctuated by the faint noise of the rest of the team warming up behind them. Beside Chrissie, Terri had suddenly become very interested in making sure her gloves were on properly, turning away a little so she didn't have to watch the two women stare each other down.

These showdowns had become such a regular occurrence at practice that most of the team saw them coming from a mile off. Chrissie was a notoriously tough coach, and Sam was a hothead who didn't take kindly to authority. It was obvious from day one that they were never going to be a match made in heaven, but for some reason, they had never settled down and gotten used to each other. They still butted heads constantly, almost like they were just looking for a reason to fight.

"I'm ten minutes late, and you're going to crucify me for that?" Sam folded her arms over her chest, narrowing her eyes at her coach. "For ten minutes?"

There it is, Chrissie thought bitterly, resisting the urge to roll her eyes. There was that Sam O'Shea sense of entitlement, just as she was expecting. She strolled onto the field with the same sense of arrogant entitlement that drove Chrissie crazy at work too—she knew she was capable, she knew she had natural skill and intelligence, and she coasted on that. At her age, Chrissie would have killed for that natural gift, that ability to intuitively know where she needed to be on the field at any given time. It was like she was made to be there.

"Get on the field, O'Shea." Chrissie took a step towards

the younger woman, closing the gap between them. At 5'6", she stood just a little shorter than Sam and had to tilt her head up ever so slightly to meet her gaze. "Don't make me ask you again."

Another beat of silence. Chrissie could practically hear the cogs whirring in Sam's mind—was it better to snap back and stomp her feet, throwing a tantrum like a child when she was told what to do or was it better just to forfeit the argument and give in?

She went with the latter. With a heavy, long-drawn-out sigh like Chrissie was asking her to move heaven and earth, she sidestepped the older woman. "Whatever you say."

Before she turned back to the team, Chrissie finally allowed herself that therapeutic eye roll. God, what a brat. It wasn't hard to believe that at one point, Sam had been a lawyer before she'd quit to become an EMT. Chrissie could see her feeling right at home in a courtroom, where she could argue just for the sake of arguing.

To give credit where it was due, once she was on the field, Sam acted like any other member of the team. She traded jokes as she warmed up, stretching out her muscles carefully so she didn't hurt herself when practice started. This was the part she took seriously; it was just a shame she didn't have that same drive and motivation to actually show up on time to practice.

Chapter 3

Practice started, and for a little while, everything was fine. It was a fairly cold October afternoon, so the team were glad to run lengths of the field, shouting instructions to each other and calling out as they chased the ball. Chrissie watched them from the sidelines, her brow furrowed in concentration as the game unfolded.

The muscles in her face twitched ever so slightly as she watched like a hawk, zeroing in on every imperfection in their form, every missed opportunity, every stupid mistake. She was a perfectionist, and it was well known that this made her a pain in the ass, but mostly, it was welcomed. Every time she barked out an instruction, the team shared knowing smiles, affectionate eye-rolls, and cracked good-natured jokes. Sure, the orders made her sound like their drill sergeant, but they came from a good place.

That was true of everyone but Sam. To say every other member of the team accepted Chrissie's criticism gladly would be a stretch, but they understood the value of it, and they knew it was coming from someone who'd spent years out on the field, doing exactly what they were doing. Sam, by contrast, seemed to take Chrissie's as though it was a personal jab.

———

Every practice ended with a cooldown exercise, while Chrissie rattled off what was wrong with their performance. For some, it was just a matter of tightening up their form, keeping their eye on the ball or making sure they were one hundred percent present in the game. For Sam, it always felt like a laundry list of problems that needed correcting.

"Adams, nice work today," Chrissie said as she passed Terri, who was stretching out her aching arms. "Other than that goal you let in."

"Nobody's perfect," Terri shot back. The two shared a knowing grin, just for a second, and then Chrissie moved on.

"O'Shea, you were sloppy today."

"Thanks, Coach," Sam muttered, dropping into a hamstring stretch. She could practically see the teleprompter in Chrissie's head whirring away, gearing up for the speech of everything that was wrong with her. Shit, wasn't soccer supposed to be *fun*? It felt like a second job with all of this criticism.

"You were supposed to be defending Terri, but you went too far out and lost the defense. It's the same thing you did last week. If you're supposed to be defending the goal, then *defend* the goal. Don't go out and play as an attacker and leave the goalkeeper wide open like that."

Chrissie moved on quickly, just as Sam's mouth opened to try to defend herself. The older woman sidestepped her, carrying on with her notes for the rest of the team, leaving Sam to stew.

"Stupid," she muttered, more to herself than to anyone else in particular. "I would've made that shot if you weren't screaming at me the entire time and distracting me."

Beside her, she heard a chuckle and glanced to her left to see Terri smiling to herself as she took off her goalkeeper's gloves. "What's so funny?"

"Nothing." Terri shrugged before meeting her gaze. "You two, I guess."

"Well, I'm glad watching me get raked over the coals for every single mistake is entertaining to you."

"It's not that," Terri assured her, pausing as Chrissie gave her wrap-up speech. It was just a few words congratulating them on a good practice and instructing them to go home and relax. Then she let them go, and they all began trekking to the locker rooms. As they walked, Terri continued. "It's not, I promise. It's just... You really are a hothead, Sam."

"I'm not a *hothead*," she defended lamely. "I'm... passionate."

Terri laughed outright at that, shaking her head. "Sure, you're passionate. That's a good way of putting it. But you let people get a rise out of you over every little thing, and that will make it tough to work with Chrissie."

"What, because she attacks you over every little mistake?"

"*No*," Terri corrected gently, stepping in to defend her old friend. "She doesn't attack anyone. Chrissie's a perfectionist, and she wants to get the best results out of us. If it feels like she's picking on you more than others, it just means she sees the wasted potential in you. And nothing gets under her skin like wasted potential. It just means she knows you can do better."

Sam pushed open the door to the locker room with a sigh. "I'm good, so she treats me like crap?"

Terri laughed at that, opening her locker. "She's not

treating you like crap. She's pushing you because she knows you can do better."

"It doesn't feel like that."

Terri glanced over at the younger blonde, who was slumped against the lockers with her arms folded, pouting like a child who'd delivered a bad report card home. "She's not doing this to be a dick, you know. She's a good person, and she cares a lot—not just about this team, but about every member of it. It's why she pushes us as much as she does. And it's why she's the one who takes on new recruits like you at work. Sure, it feels like you've signed up for the army at the time, but you come out of it better, trust me."

Sam hummed out something that sounded like vague agreement. "Any tips on how to survive her?"

Terri smiled, just a little. "Don't let her get a rise out of you. Chill out, take a step back, and just listen to what she's saying. Sooner or later, you'll realize she's not bullying you, she's just pushing you."

Sam was quiet as the older woman started getting changed. *Was Terri right? Was Chrissie just pushing her?*

Chapter 4

"I need a new partner."

Steve O'Reilly was tired. He was *always* tired and had been since he'd ended his probation as an EMT what felt like a lifetime ago. But Chrissie Woods had a unique way of sucking out whatever dregs of energy were floating around in his body still. Somehow, no matter whether it was a positive or negative one, every meeting with her left him drained.

It was Tuesday morning, and the day shift hadn't even started yet. But Chrissie had found her way into his office, demanding his attention in a way no one else would ever dare. The boss-employee relationship seemed a little skewed out of his favor when it came to Chrissie.

He leaned back in his desk chair slowly, listening to the plastic creak in protest under his weight. He and Chrissie had worked together for five years, ever since she'd transferred to his station, and they'd developed a strange sort of friendship over that time. Sure, she wasn't his first choice in a drinking partner on a Saturday night, but there was a lot of mutual respect there.

"Good morning, Steve." He pitched his voice a little higher, mimicking her voice. "How was your weekend?"

Chrissie's lips pursed into a thin white line as she folded her arms over her chest. Inhaling slowly, she parroted his words back to him.

"Good morning, Steve. How was your weekend?"

He wasn't done though. "Wasn't it your anniversary with your wife this weekend? Did you do anything nice, did you maybe spend the weekend away together? That must have been nice."

That earned him a heavy sigh. "Steve, cut the crap."

"You cut the crap," he shot back, straightening up in his chair. "You aren't getting a new partner."

"Because I didn't ask you about your anniversary?"

"Yes, Chrissie," he deadpanned. "I won't give you a new partner because you were rude to me. I'm that good of a boss."

"I'm serious. I need a new partner. I can't keep working with O'Shea."

Steve fished a pen from the pot on his desk, popping it into his mouth like a cigarette. It was an old habit he'd started when he'd quit smoking a few years earlier, and now he did it without even realizing half the time.

"Why not?" he asked finally, swinging back in the chair again. "She kill a patient?"

"No."

"Then, why?"

"Because she's a fucking brat, that's why. I didn't become an EMT so I could hand feed her with the silver spoon she came in here with."

Steve's eyebrows shot up at her remark. Over the years she'd spent as an EMT, Chrissie had become a begrudging maternal figure for many of the younger EMTs. It was an unspoken rule that the fresh-faced new recruits would spend a rotation with her while they settled into their new roles. As blunt and no-nonsense as she was, Chrissie had a soft spot for the EMTs on probation.

They'd had new recruits who didn't last. Recruits who got into the job for the wrong reasons, couldn't adjust to the pressure of the job, or couldn't handle seeing so much death on a day to day basis. Chrissie had stood beside so many of those young recruits, held so many hands as they cried over their first losses. And she'd never once reacted like this.

That was why it had made complete sense to Steve to put Sam with her when she joined the team. She was young, she was eager to learn the ropes, and she was whip-smart. Chrissie had taken care of so many kids that had turned pale at the sight of blood, or who had panicked under the slightest pressure; Steve had thought a recruit who seemed more naturally capable would be the perfect fit.

"'The silver spoon she came in here with'?" he echoed slowly, shaking his head in disbelief. "Shit, remind me never to piss you off."

"I need a new partner," Chrissie repeated, more forcefully this time. Steve threw his hands up in a 'what can I do?' gesture.

"Of course, let me rearrange everyone's schedules and waste my morning to satisfy your needs."

"I'm serious, Steve."

"So am I." It wasn't often Steve put his foot down as Chrissie's boss. In truth, there was a small part of him—just a small part—that was a little afraid of her. She reminded him of his mother, and not necessarily in a complimentary way. Nonetheless, on this, he wasn't going to give in. "This station doesn't operate according to your every whim. I'm not changing everyone's rotas just because you've got a problem with O'Shea."

"She's a pain in the ass."

"Fuck, Chrissie, and you're *not?*"

She opened her mouth to argue back, but whatever response she had died on her lips, and she closed her mouth again, looking defeated. Steve had no idea what her problem really was with the younger recruit, and although he was curious, he didn't have the luxury of time to waste figuring it out.

"Make it work," he suggested, motioning to Chrissie with his pen. "You've made it work with countless newbies before —kids who were dumber than O'Shea and more of a pain in the ass. So I don't care what personal shit you're dealing with, but can it, and focus on the patients. You got that?"

He saw anger flare up in her face at that. They'd worked together long enough that the occasional personal favor under the table was never a particularly big deal to either of them. Sometimes Chrissie got vacations approved faster than newer recruits, sometimes Steve got tips on the women's soccer matches so he could win some cash with his bookie. Sure, it wasn't necessarily fair, but it was one of the few perks of their relationship. Obviously, she thought this would be a chance for her to call in another favor from Steve, but today he wasn't going to bite.

"What is this about, anyway?" he asked, his natural curiosity winning out. This was by no means the first time Chrissie had come to his office to complain about a new recruit he'd paired her up with. She'd often throw herself down in the chair across from him and roll off some spiel about her newest partner, before composing herself and settling into a routine with them over time. But this was different. This was the first time she'd ever asked for a new partner. What was different about Sam?

There was a beat of silence as Chrissie shifted from foot to foot, trying to come up with something specific that bothered her about Sam. Steve's eyes narrowed. "This had better not be about soccer."

He knew about Chrissie's team. He knew Sam played for that team, and he had it on good authority that their relationship on the field was no better than their relationship in the back of an ambulance.

"It's not about soccer!"

"I swear to christ, Chrissie," he began, pointing at her with his pen again. "If you're busting into my office this early because she pissed you off at practice…"

"It's not about practice!" Chrissie snapped, throwing her hands up in the air.

A few seconds passed while they glared at each other. It was obvious he didn't believe her, and eventually, his icy stare wore her down, just a little. "It's not *just* about practice."

That was all Steve needed. He tossed the pen down on his desk decisively. "No new partner. Whatever problems the two of you have, figure them out on your own time. Don't bring your shit into work, just focus on your patients. You got it?"

She wanted to argue back. He could see it written all over her face, from the way her brown eyes narrowed, to the little flare of her nostrils. A few seconds passed, and eventually she breathed out a heavy sigh.

"Fine."

Steve felt himself relax a little in his chair. Good. He wasn't ready for a fight, not this early on a Tuesday morning, and definitely not with Chrissie Woods.

He checked the clock on the wall. "You're on shift. You should get back to work."

"Thanks for the help, boss," she muttered, turning on her heel and leaving. There was a cold venom to her words that almost made him wince, and if it had been anyone else, Steve probably would have pulled them up on it. He let her leave though, and when the door swung shut behind her, he sank down in his chair.

Seriously, what was the deal with those two?

<hr>

Chapter 5

<hr>

For the next two days, things didn't seem quite so bad between the two of them. Chrissie, ever the professional, tried her hardest to get along with the younger recruit. Every time Chrissie felt a sharp criticism rise, every time she heard a muttered comment from Sam, Steve's words echoed in her head about playing nice, and she calmed herself down.

She even tried to carry that over into their mid-week soccer practice, and her efforts didn't go unnoticed. When Sam showed up late to the field, Chrissie waited patiently for her excuse rather than snapping at the younger woman, even though it was apparent to everyone that she was struggling a little. Sam seemed to appreciate it, and for the first time in a long while, practice flew by without any major incidents between them. There were no fights, there were no sarcastic comments, and it was a pleasant change of pace for everyone.

It didn't last.

Strictly speaking, as Terri informed Chrissie later over a couple of beers, the fight was *her* fault, not Sam's. If Chrissie was being honest, she knew that was the case, but she still refused to shoulder the blame entirely.

They were on the late shift together, which was a recipe for disaster even under the best of circumstances. But, when coupled with the shitty morning Chrissie had dragged herself through before even getting into work, it was sure to be a complete nightmare.

Her day had started pretty well, with coffee and a leftover doughnut for breakfast. But pretty much everything that happened after that was set to raise Chrissie's blood pressure sky-high.

She should have known it was going to be a shitty day when she saw the caller ID of her ex light up on her phone, just as she was finishing breakfast. After six months, the memory of the woman she'd planned on one day marrying just walking out of her life was still a relatively fresh cut on her heart, and seeing her name flash up on the screen reopened the wound.

Chrissie hadn't spoken to Charlotte since the night she'd come home from work to a hallway full of boxes, a guilty-looking ex-girlfriend, and a bullshit apology speech about how she needed to find herself. A tiny part of her lived in the hope that one day her ex would come around and remember how good they'd had it together, and her life would go back to normal, but that day had never happened.

When she picked up the phone, it was with that same cautious optimism, which was almost immediately dashed when she realized why Charlotte was calling. It turned out that when she'd packed up all of her things and walked out, she'd ended up leaving behind some paychecks in a shoebox under the bed, which she needed for her taxes. She wanted Chrissie to mail them to her at her new address.

She half-heartedly offered to drive them over and deliver them in person before work, but Charlotte quickly stopped her.

"No, no, just send them over. That's fine."

As she spoke, Chrissie heard another woman talking in the background. Her voice was muffled, but she managed to make out a few things. Namely, she was asking Charlotte what she wanted for dinner that night, and then she heard 'baby'.

Her stomach twisted into knots almost immediately. That was why Charlotte wanted the paychecks mailed, not delivered. She didn't want Chrissie to see how quickly she'd been replaced with someone new, how happy she now was. How she'd managed to 'find herself'.

"Sure," she managed to choke out. "I'll send them over tomorrow."

By the time she'd arrived at work later that day for her shift with Sam, Chrissie had been looking for a fight. She knew it was childish; she knew it was wrong, but she was *pissed*, and she was tired of biting her tongue and playing nice with Sam and getting nothing in return.

It was obvious she was in a foul mood from the moment she stepped through the doors. There was practically a thundercloud of misery hanging over her—a good metaphor for the storm that was about to come. Word got around pretty quickly that *something* was up with Chrissie, though no one was quite sure what.

Sam was in the locker room, getting into uniform, when she too heard about Chrissie's foul mood.

"Chrissie's in." Terri appeared beside her, startling her. How the other woman managed to have a knack for sneaking around so quietly was totally beyond her.

"Not really surprising, seeing as how we're on shift together today."

Terri leaned against the wall with one shoulder, evaluating Sam slowly, like she was trying to gauge how she was feeling. "Try not to piss her off today."

"I never *try* to—"

"You know what I mean," Terri cut across her. "Don't do anything that'll get under her skin. She's...been having a rough morning."

Sam resisted the almost overwhelming urge to roll her eyes. When wasn't Chrissie having a rough morning? It seemed like every other week there was something new pissing her off. Sam was pretty sure she'd only seen the older woman smile on a handful of occasions during her time as an EMT—and one of those was when they'd delivered a new baby into the world.

"I'm just asking you to cut her some slack today." Terri opened her own locker, grabbing her things. She'd been on the day shift, and finally she was allowed to kick off her boots and go home. "She might be a little..."

"A little what?"

"Well, a little more..." Terri searched for the right word. "Chrissie-y than normal."

Sam exhaled slowly in an attempt to mentally ready herself for the evening ahead. After thanking Terri for the heads up about her senior's mood, Sam headed off towards the bay, looking for that familiar head of short brown hair.

Chapter 6

Chrissie sat staring at her phone when Sam clambered into the cab beside her. It was the same page of local news that filled her screen now as it had been when she first tapped the screen over fifteen minutes ago and she still hadn't read a word.

"Evening, Chrissie," Sam said quietly, closing the door behind her as she settled into the seat.

Chrissie grunted. She wasn't in the mood for the younger woman's entitled attitude today. Thankfully, perhaps because she sensed Chrissie's short temper, Sam kept quiet.

The first couple of cases weren't so bad. The first call-out was for a case that turned out to be nothing more than an idiot who had a minor burn on his hand. Chrissie managed to get a little of the frustration out of her system by telling him that a small burn that he'd managed to get while taking his frozen pizza out of the oven wasn't a life-or-death situation. The next case was a pregnant woman who was going into labor, and they had to work so quickly that there was little time to stop and talk.

The third case was the one that prompted the fight.

It was a suspected drug overdose, a patient who was barely coherent when they arrived at his shoebox apartment, kicking their way through takeout boxes and beer cans to get to him. There were needles nearby, and it was evident that he was having an adverse reaction.

Chrissie was barely fazed by scenes like that anymore. Her brain seemed to kick into a higher gear when she put on the uniform, and while seeing an addict passed out from drugs was sad, it didn't necessarily affect her the way it used to. She dealt with it the way she dealt with every case—calm, collected, ever the professional.

Sam, though? She was like a Labrador puppy who hadn't been fully trained yet. She jumped into the job headfirst, the same way she approached almost everything. It was like she had tunnel vision, and all she could see was what was directly in front of her. Sure, maybe that was great for a penalty shootout on the field, but when juggling how to treat a drug overdose, a little more care was needed.

It was that tunnel vision of Sam's that started the argument. She dove straight in, ready to treat the patient immediately, without even bothering to take a quick glance in the medicine cabinet like Chrissie did. That was where she found the medication for the heart problem the patient had —the heart problem that probably would have spiraled into a full-blown heart attack if Sam had managed to successfully administer the treatment she wanted to.

What happened after Chrissie barked at Sam to *stop* was a little hazy. Maybe she snapped at the younger recruit. Perhaps she was a bit too harsh. She honestly couldn't remember either way, but she did know that the drive to the hospital to drop him off in the ER was a silent one.

They had a few quiet minutes after dropping that patient off at City General, so they hit the drive-through and got some coffee, sitting in the parking lot of a nearby McDonald's for a short break. That was when Chrissie made the mistake of bringing up Sam's attention to detail (or lack of it).

She wasn't trying to be overly critical when she brought it up. She just wanted to offer some words of wisdom, from one EMT to another. But maybe that lingering frustration from the conversation with Charlotte was still hanging around her. Perhaps that was why it came out more like she was telling Sam off than giving her advice.

"You need to be more careful when you go into cases like that. You need to stop and take a second to look around and see the big picture rather than jumping in headfirst."

Chrissie watched as Sam picked at the rim of her to-go coffee cup, bending the plastic a little under her nail. There was something in the way the young woman fidgeted that betrayed the frustration she appeared to be biting back.

"I'll bear that in mind, thanks."

"I'm not saying the treatment was wrong. For any other patient, you would have been making the right move, but you missed something vital. If I hadn't picked up on it—"

"I get it, thanks, Chrissie," she said coolly. "I nearly killed someone tonight. Thanks."

And just like that, with those few words, all of the tension that they'd managed to hold at bay over the last few days came flooding back into the cab of the ambulance. For a moment, the only sound that permeated the air was that of the traffic on the road nearby, and then Chrissie broke the silence.

"This is serious, O'Shea. You need to pay attention to details like this because if you don't, there could be serious problems."

"You've made it clear that you think I'm shit at this job," Sam snapped back. "I get it. Without Saint Chrissie stepping in, he would have died. Well, thank you for covering my ass."

"Christ, Sam!" she cried out. "You think this is me trying to one-up you?"

"No, I think maybe you like to find something wrong with every little thing I do. I don't know, maybe that's what gets you off. Maybe you like making me feel like shit about the work that I do. Is that it?"

"Did you ever think that maybe I'm finding something wrong with everything you do because you keep fucking up in front of me?"

Whatever response Sam was about to come up with was cut short when the radio crackled to life. They had another job, only a short drive away, but from the sounds of things, it was serious.

The argument went on the back burner as they tossed their empty coffee cups in the trash and headed to their next call. Chrissie could sense Sam's glare as she pulled the truck out into the road, sirens blaring.

Chapter 7

It might not have been so bad if they'd been able to forget about the fight when their shift ended. They had some time apart before soccer practice the next afternoon, so if they'd been able to put it to rest, things might not have escalated.

Maybe they were both just too stubborn to do that though, or perhaps they both genuinely believed the other was the one in the wrong. Either way, when practice started the next afternoon, any chance of either one acting cordially went out of the window.

It was worse than normal, and everyone could see it. Sam wasn't playing to her usual standard—she was getting sloppy, missing shots that she ordinarily could have made with her eyes closed, and generally not even bothering to try. The whole team could see something was wrong, and her behavior didn't go unnoticed by the coach, either.

The shrill call of the whistle halted practice when there were only twenty minutes left to go, and Chrissie actually stepped onto the field to get involved.

"O'Shea," she snapped, pointing a finger at the blonde as

she crossed the field. Sam stood towards the back, hanging close to Terri's goal. "What are you doing?"

"Playing defense, Coach." She folded her arms. "Just like you told me to."

"I didn't tell you to stand there and do nothing." Chrissie came right up to her, gesturing around at Sam's teammates. "You're supposed to be supporting them."

"I have been." Sam gestured to the mud that flecked her clothes and face as though this was a sign of her involvement in the game. It had been raining during the day, and every time they kicked the ball, they were flicking mud all over themselves. Chrissie was far too experienced a coach to be fooled by a splatter of mud. She'd watched Sam and her half-hearted effort.

"If you aren't going to bother playing, then get off the field," she snapped. This wasn't an unfamiliar threat—once or twice a month *someone* heard that phrase. She never actually meant that she wanted her players to leave—it was her way of saying 'pick up the slack', and it always had the desired effect.

Not today, though. Instead of hearing 'Yes, Coach', or 'Sorry, Coach', like usual, she saw a flash of anger cross over the young blonde's face. No one spoke, and the heavy silence between them seemed to drag on for an eternity as though Sam was deciding her next move.

Finally, grabbing the bib, Sam tore it off. "Okay," was all she said, dropping the bib at Chrissie's feet. Around them, there were hushed whispers of shock. In all the time Chrissie had been coaching the team, no one had *ever* walked off in the middle of a game, no matter how bad the fight was.

Sam stormed off the field towards the changing rooms, head high, not looking at any of her teammates. No one went after her, and even Chrissie didn't yell her name. Instead, she surprised everyone by calling practice to an early end.

"Everyone just go home. That's enough for today," she said quietly, picking up Sam's bib from the mud. Confused, the rest of the team made their way to the locker room, following Sam's lead. Eventually, only Terri and Chrissie were left on the field.

"Fucking brat," Chrissie hissed, looking at the bib in her hands. "Who does she think she is, god's gift to soccer?"

Terri took off her own bib, handing it over more kindly than her teammate. "So things are going well then?"

"Oh, things are going fucking *swimmingly*, can't you tell?"

"You two really do know how to get under each other's skin, don't you?" Terri looked past Chrissie to the locker rooms, following the path Sam had taken.

"She's annoying."

"So am I, but we don't fight like that," Terri commented. Chrissie was still looking down at the bib, so she didn't notice the knowing smile that crossed her friend's lips. "Actually, I think I've only seen you fight like this with one other person before."

That caught Chrissie's attention. Her head shot up, and her eyes narrowed. "Who?"

Instead of answering, Terri just smiled then walked away heading for the locker room to join her teammates.

"Who, Terri?"

Without turning around, Terri threw up one arm to wave goodbye. "I'll see you at work!"

Chapter 8

Sam was taking her time getting out of her uniform after she left the field. It didn't take long for the rest of the team to filter in, and the usual post-practice energy that normally filled the room was gone. That hollow emptiness in the locker room, coupled with the fact that she knew everyone was looking at her out of the corner of their eye, made getting changed a little difficult.

Eventually, everyone left, and she was alone in the locker room with her thoughts. She was still stewing over the fight from before, still bitter and angry about what Chrissie had said to her in the ambulance. She opened up her locker, wanting nothing more than to get into her regular clothes, head home and get drunk on that cheap wine in her fridge, but then the door swung open behind her.

"O'Shea."

Of course, Sam thought bitterly, stopping herself as she reached for her clean clothes. *Of course Chrissie would wait until everyone else has gone so that she can scream at me as much as she wants.*

"What do you want?" Sam snapped, almost surprising

herself at how cold her voice was. In the reflection of the mirror on the inside of her locker door, she caught sight of Chrissie's face and saw her eyebrows shoot up a little, taken aback by her tone.

It didn't take long for Chrissie to snap back into her normal routine, though.

"You need to get it together," she barked, stepping forward until she was in Sam's personal space. In the cramped space, Sam turned to look up at her, managing to muster up the energy to glare at her. After a twelve hour shift where she did nothing but get yelled at by her senior, she then had to get bullied by her during practice too.

So much for being a professional.

Sam was too exhausted for this. She was flecked with mud, her muscles ached—whether it was from the game or from the patients during the day, she had no idea—and she didn't have it in her to feel Chrissie's wrath yet again.

"What do you mean 'get it together'?" she echoed, hearing her voice raise in anger, just a little bit.

Terri's voice rang in the back of her head. *Don't let her get a rise out of you.*

She didn't have the energy to restrain herself right now, though. Right now, what she wanted was a nice hot shower before falling into bed, and Chrissie was the only obstacle blocking her from that.

"You're a better player than this, you know that, right?" Chrissie's tone was even and composed, and if it hadn't been for the slight flex in her jaw Sam could have sworn the older woman was trying to be friendly. *But fuck that.*

"You've got a natural talent. A talent that most people would kill to have but you're so focused on thinking you're getting a raw deal you're acting like a jackass," Chrissie said.

"A jackass?" Sam's nostrils flared, and she drew herself up to her full height with a sharp breath.

"You want me to give you the whole speech again?" Chrissie asked. "You want me to tell you how you're wasting your potential, letting your talent rot while you skate through this?"

Sam tossed the half-empty water bottle down on the nearby bench. In the otherwise silent room, the clatter of plastic on wood echoed loudly, like a warning bell for the shouting match that was about to start.

"I'm not skating through shit, Chrissie!"

Don't let her get a rise out of you. Terri's words were just a whisper now.

There was a beat of silence as the older woman looked her up and down. Clenching and unclenching her hands, she was aware of the blisters and calluses from moving patients around all day and the sensitive skin that surrounded the bruises which covered her knees from the number of falls she'd taken. She was hardly skating. But even so, Chrissie wouldn't back down.

"You don't apply yourself. You think because you're naturally *good*, you can just relax. You miss things because you get cocky, just like you missed that pass on the field, just like you missed that heart problem this—"

"*Don't* bring that up."

"You missed it though, didn't you?" Chrissie took one last step forwards until she was practically nose-to-nose with Sam. "And if I hadn't spotted it, we'd have lost the patient. How much longer am I going to have to keep cleaning up your messes, O'Shea?"

"*Fuck you.*"

Her words hung in the air, and for a moment, it was like they were echoing over and over in the tiny room, bouncing off the tiles until it was all Sam could hear.

Then something seemed to snap between them. They were both pissed off, topped up on adrenaline, and suddenly their eyes locked and then without a word passing between them it was as though they both felt the bolt of electricity suddenly making only one thing that made sense to them both.

Sam would have been lying if she said she'd never thought about kissing the older woman before. It had happened a few times—she'd catch herself thinking about Chrissie while watching Netflix, or while she was waiting in the queue for her coffee in the morning. But never once had she imagined this would be how it would go.

Thinking back on it later, neither of them would be quite sure who made the first move, but at that moment, it didn't matter. It was just the only thing that made sense; the only thing that said everything neither of them could put into words.

Chapter 9

There was nothing gentle with her touch as Chrissie pushed Sam back against the lockers, one hand on the small of her back and the other clutching onto her hip. When Chrissie pulled back, just for a few seconds, she looked at the younger woman and almost didn't recognize her. Her pupils were blown wide, her lips were swollen and red, and her chest rose and fell like she was in the middle of a game. They paused, just for a moment, and Chrissie's hand curled into the fabric of Sam's shirt, tugging it up just a little. Her eyebrows raised in a silent question.

Is this okay?

"Take it off." Sam's voice was ragged and raw when she spoke, and the words came out somewhere between an order and begging—Chrissie couldn't be sure which it sounded like. Either way, how could Chrissie not comply?

The shirt and sports bra came off, pulled over her head and discarded on the floor. As if in a mixture of exposure and anticipation, Sam's nipples hardened. She drew Chrissie back into a rougher, harder kiss, both women hungry for each other. Chrissie's hands hooked under the waistband of Sam's shorts, her fingers ghosting over the cotton.

"Chrissie, take them *off.*"

Again, Sam may have been trying to make it sound like an order, but that desperate whine gave it away—she was begging. She seemed to need this so badly, Chrissie couldn't help but wonder how long it had been for her.

"Sam, I... "

"Chrissie, please. I want you. Take them *off, now.*"

Wasting no more time, Chrissie slid Sam's shorts and underwear down, pausing only to allow Sam to kick off her boots. Her hands slid over her smooth, tanned skin, aware of how shallow her breathing had become. As Sam stood in front of her naked, she took in her toned, sculpted body. She had imagined her body many times as she'd watched her play, and each time she chastised herself, shaking the image out of her head and focusing on the game in hand. But Sam was more beautiful than she had imagined.

Chrissie was lost in wonder, but as Sam grabbed her shirt and pulled her in, she came back into the moment, aware of Sam's tugging to remove her top. Within minutes they were both naked, reveling in the contact of skin on skin. Sam, grabbing Chrissie's ass, lifted her across to the wide benches that sat in the middle of the locker room. She placed her down with such care it caused Chrissie to smile.

"You're not going to get soft on me now are you?" Without waiting for an answer, she placed her lips on Sam's and groaned in delight as she was pinned down, allowing her to take complete control.

Sam's hand brushed past the side of her breast and with featherlight grace, it slid down her body and over her thighs, causing Chrissie to shudder in anticipation. As Sam trailed her fingertips over the soft flesh of her inner thigh, Chrissie whimpered in response, causing her own excitement to pulse through her veins.

The heat as Sam's fingers made their way through Chrissie's short trimmed hair into her wetness was intoxicating. All rationale had been abandoned, and neither could stop themselves. The simmering desire which both had refused to acknowledge for so long had now been unleashed, and nothing was going to stop them until they were satiated.

Chrissie felt fingers slide over her swollen clit; she groaned with pleasure as those two fingers deftly slipped deep inside, pushing hard. Her eyes locked with Sam's and the intensity of desire increased. She had never wanted to be taken so much. Sam held her body tightly in place, and as Chrissie tried to rise, pushing against her hand to take her deeper still, it was Sam who was in charge.

Chrissie lost control; coming hard, fast, and tightly around Sam's hand as she surrendered to her unrelenting rhythm. As tremors ran through Chrissie's body, Sam lowered herself down. She sucked in a breath, shaking as Sam's lips sucked in her clit, teasing and whipping with a tense tongue. Fingers filled her and all too quickly the rise of a second orgasm started to build. Gushing in appreciation, she closed her eyes and lost her body to a thousand tremors of delight.

As her eyes fluttered open, it was the sight of Sam's firm breasts lowering over her, as she aimed for her mouth, which pitched her hunger again. This time she wanted to taste the woman who had just brought her so much pleasure. Pulling her down tight on top of her, she rolled her over, swapping positions. Straddling her, she grabbed Sam's wrists, pinning her hands above her head, kissing her roughly. She had never seen so much want in anyone's eyes. Slowly, she allowed her eyes to take in the full beauty that lay before her. She bit down on her bottom lip, filled with the thrill of what lay ahead. Lifting her weight from Sam, she raised herself up to standing and held out a hand to her.

"Turn over. I want you on all fours."

A carnal desire overtook Chrissie, and as soon as Sam had positioned herself, she ran her hands over her butt and into her core. As Sam groaned with pleasure, Chrissie threw her head back, closing her eyes and allowing the burst of excitement to fill her chest before thrusting two fingers deep inside. Her tempo was powerful and consistent, causing Sam to push back, arching and aching for more.

"Harder." Sam's tone was not one of order but begging, and it sent a pulse of excitement through Chrissie.

Responding with vigor, she immediately felt Sam tighten around her fingers. Losing no time, she slid her free hand over Sam's butt and around the top of her thigh until her fingers found her throbbing clit. The powerful circles and strokes were enough to send Sam toppling into a deep guttural moan before her body descended into orgasm.

Chrissie leant over her, placing small kisses up her spine and holding her loosely. Breathing heavily with satisfaction, their thirst quenched, the spell was lifted. They pulled apart, and an awkwardness immediately filled the air. Neither of them quite knew what to say.

All the normal pillow talk options seemed a little forced or perverse after what had just happened. They got dressed in silence, avoiding making eye contact as they gathered their things, and when they were both fully clothed, a heavy silence hung between them.

The air felt hot and humid, a stark reminder of what they'd just done. When Chrissie cleared her throat to speak, the words died in her throat. She had no idea what she was supposed to say here, so after a moment of struggling to find something—*anything*—to express what was racing through her head, she just closed her mouth again.

Sam appeared just as awkward, choosing to avert her eyes as she crouched down focusing on tying the laces of her sneakers. Her hair fell around her face in a tangled veil, but it still didn't hide her flushed cheeks from Chrissie.

Finally, Chrissie broke the uncomfortable silence. "I'll see you at work tomorrow."

Her voice didn't sound like her own. It was quiet, tiny, and barely carried across the small room, but she couldn't bring herself to say anything more. Sam just hummed out something that sounded like 'okay'. And with that, the older woman left.

The door swung shut behind Chrissie, and Sam waited in silence as her footsteps got fainter and fainter. Eventually, they faded into nothing, and that was when she let out the shaky breath she hadn't even realized she was holding in. She fell backwards, so she was propped up against the lockers, and her eyes closed slowly while her heartbeat returned to normal.

"Was that a mistake?" she whispered to the empty room. On the one hand, she couldn't shake that guilty feeling deep in her stomach, as if they'd just crossed some previously unacknowledged line and broken some kind of rule that someone had laid down.

On the other hand, when Sam's hand dropped to her chest, and her fingertips massaged into the fabric of her shirt just below her clavicle, she couldn't help the tiny smile that tugged at her lips. Underneath that shirt there was a blossoming bruise left by Chrissie's lips—a reminder that she'd see and feel for the rest of the week. And it was a reminder that didn't feel wrong at all. It was a reminder she was glad to have, in a strange way. It was a reminder of how good it had felt when Chrissie had kissed her, how she'd made Sam move and react in ways she had forgotten were possible.

That was the thing they both came to realize that night, when they were both at home, staring at the ceiling late at night. They traced patterns over their skin where the other had touched, their fingers leaving expectant goosebumps in their wake. It hadn't felt wrong at the time, they realized.

In fact, in the moment, even with how sweaty and desperate and messy it was, it had felt so *right*, just for those few minutes.

Chapter 10

It was two days before they saw each other again and although they both had ways to get in contact with the other, neither picked up the phone. Neither one of them tried to bridge that gap, even though it was the only thing either of them thought about.

In fact, they managed to make it the whole way through a shift together without bringing it up. Things seemed pretty much the same as they had done before the locker room, except for the stolen glances across the cab of the truck when they thought the other wasn't looking.

It wasn't until the end of their shift, when they were in the parking lot about to head home that they brought up what had happened. Sam was the one to do it.

"So, what now?" she asked, stopping Chrissie before the older woman opened the door of her car. "Do we just... Go back to doing what we were doing? Hatefuck every so often when we piss each other off?"

Chrissie frowned at her choice of phrasing, but said nothing. What was she supposed to say? There were so many reasons that the two of them made a terrible couple that she didn't even know where to begin. There was the age gap—Chrissie was in her thirties while Sam was in her twenties, with all the hot-headed powerful energy that came at that age. There was the still-tender wound left by Charlotte leaving Chrissie—she wasn't ready to open herself back up to that kind of emotional connection again, and risk that kind of pain. And then there was the fact that they drove each other fucking *crazy*, and not always in a good way.

Her silence said everything she couldn't. Chrissie watched as a series of emotions crossed over Sam's face, each so quick that she would have missed them if they hadn't been so pronounced. There was cautious optimism, confusion, realization, and then overwhelming hurt.

"I guess not."

"Sam…" Chrissie sighed. "How would this work? Tell me how it would work with… Everything."

"How does *anything* work? I don't know, that's why people take risks!"

Chrissie let out a sharp bark of hoarse laughter. "Exactly. That just proves my point. I'm thirty-six, I'm done taking risks. I was done a long time ago."

"So you're being a coward, is that it?"

Chrissie glared at her. Sure, she didn't necessarily expect Sam to understand precisely what she was feeling right now —at twenty-four years old. How many heartbreaks could she have had? But even so, she'd expected a little empathy.

"That's not what this is."

The younger blonde rolled her eyes, managing to choke out a mirthless laugh. "Sure, whatever."

Chrissie wanted to say something. She *should* have said something—anything—to get Sam to stop and listen. She should have tried to explain herself, but for some reason, nothing came out of her mouth. She just stood there, struck dumb by some overpowering force while Sam unlocked her car and drove off, burning rubber on the tarmac in her haste to leave.

That night while she stared up at the ceiling, a whole speech came to her. It explained everything: the fear of getting involved with someone again after Charlotte, the age difference, the problems with getting involved with a co-worker. It came too late though—on their next shift, Sam wouldn't even look at her unless they had a patient, and even then it seemed like she was looking *through* Chrissie rather than at her.

That was what hurt the most, Chrissie realized. That rejection, that complete disregard. It stung more than she could have imagined and made her feel even more guilty.

Something changed between them in the next few weeks, though no one else could quite put their finger on what could have made the difference. Everyone around them saw it, but no one dared to comment. Even Terri kept her mouth shut.

When Sam showed up late to practice, Chrissie didn't pull her up on it. Where she would have rolled her eyes, huffed out something about Sam being unprofessional and wasting her time, now there was none of that. She let Sam breeze onto the field ten or fifteen minutes after everyone else without a word. Hell, she barely even *looked* at the girl now.

Chrissie didn't bother asking for another partner again. She couldn't give a good reason for wanting a new partner, and she knew she could never explain everything that had happened between her and Sam. So instead, she just had to grit her teeth and bear the silent treatment she was being given.

It had been almost a month since the incident in the locker room when they got the call out about the three-car pile-up. The radio crackled to life on an otherwise silent late November evening, and as they were the closest, they responded to it.

Two cars had collided on the road—it looked like one had rear-ended the other, and the second car had ended up in the embankment. They were the first to arrive, and for a few moments, Chrissie was so focused on getting to the patients that she didn't notice Sam lagging behind.

The smell of a leaking gas tank was what hit her first. As she clambered out of the ambulance, Sam felt a wave of nausea sweep over her that stopped her in her tracks. For a few seconds, the cars in front of her vanished, and Chrissie, who was calling her name, disappeared. For just a few moments, she wasn't watching a crash from the outside; she was trapped inside it, screaming herself hoarse.

"Mom?"

The fumes were overpowering, and as Sam took a stumbling step forward, she could feel the phantom pain of the seatbelt cutting into her chest, just as it had done the night of the crash.

"Mom?!"

She could feel bile rising in the back of her throat as the crash in front of her blurred, and she couldn't tell what was in front of her from the memories she was struggling to escape from. Her heart was racing, beating so hard and so fast that as she stood there, she was convinced she could hear it.

"O'Shea!"

Chrissie's voice cut through the haze, and slowly, Sam felt

herself come back to reality. She blinked once, and the smell of gasoline started to fade. Once more, and she was back to reality.

She wasn't trapped in the mangled wreckage of a car. She wasn't screaming in vain for a dead woman. She wasn't a survivor, desperately praying for rescue. Tonight, she was part of the rescue team.

"Sam, I need you over here!" Chrissie was crouched by the car, staring up at her with wide eyes, pleading with her. Sam shook herself sternly, and forced herself to put one shaky foot in front of the other, until eventually, after what seemed like an age, she ended up beside Chrissie in front of the car.

"What do we have?" she asked. Her voice was hoarse, ragged and raw, and it didn't sound like it was coming out of her. Sam could tell the older woman was trying to figure out what was going on with her, but she didn't have time to ask.

"Two females, conscious and responsive, but injured."

Somewhere through the fog, Sam managed to register and process that information, and slowly, she managed to respond. Afterwards, once the two young women (college students, they later found out) were in the ER being treated for minor wounds, she remembered nothing. No matter how hard she tried to piece together what had happened at the scene of the crash, all she could think of was the smell of gasoline.

And Chrissie.

Despite remembering nothing else about the crash after they arrived on the scene, Sam could remember Chrissie. She could remember the sound of Chrissie's voice, gently guiding her through the fog, even if she couldn't recall the exact words.

Was this what she was going to be like with every crash? Every time she was needed to help with victims of a road accident, would she freeze like a deer in headlights? Would she get trapped back in the front seat of her mother's car again and again?

How could she think of herself as an EMT if that was the future for her? How could she possibly help people if she was this helpless?

Chapter 11

Chrissie was worried.

She'd wanted to talk to Sam about what had happened at the scene of the crash, but during the drive back to the station, the blonde seemed like she was in a trance. She was acting on autopilot through the whole job, and once the two college girls were in the hospital, it was like she just shut down.

When they got back to the station, Chrissie tried to talk to her, but the blonde disappeared in the direction of Steve's office, and Chrissie decided it was best to give her some space for the time being. That was until Steve found her not long after.

"What happened on the shift?" he asked, more concerned than annoyed. As it turned out, Sam had wandered into his office without knocking and told him to expect her resignation letter. That was all she'd said before walking off, leaving Steve more than a little confused. So now Chrissie was looking for her.

She wasn't in the locker room, which was where Chrissie

checked first. She wasn't in the bathrooms either, and by the time Chrissie finally made it out to the parking lot, her car was gone. So now she was chasing Sam back to her house, desperate to try to talk to her and find out exactly what was going on.

It took Sam a while to open the door, despite how loudly Chrissie was knocking. When she finally answered, she was still dressed in her uniform. Her skin was blotchy, and her eyes were rimmed red like she'd been crying.

"Hi," was all she said.

For some reason, that annoyed Chrissie more than anything. That was the first thing she'd said to Chrissie that didn't have anything to do with work in almost a month, and after everything, those two letters were all she could muster? Was that all Chrissie was worth?

"What's this shit about you quitting?" Chrissie pushed her way into the front hallway, letting the door close behind her. "Is your head so far up your own ass that you have to quit after one bad day?"

Shockingly, Sam didn't rise to the bait. There was no tell-tale flare of the nostrils. She didn't draw herself up to her full height, and she didn't say anything in return. It was like all the fight had drained out of her.

"It wasn't just one bad day," she whispered, walking into the front room before dropping onto the couch with a shaky sigh. "I know it wasn't."

"What do you mean?" Chrissie followed her, hearing her voice soften as she spoke. "That was the first time you ever—"

"It won't be the only time." Sam shook her head slowly, tears sparkling in her eyes. "I just... I can't. That crash felt *real*."

"Sam, what are you talking about?" Chrissie whispered. She had the sudden urge to reach out and take the blonde's hand, but she resisted. After all, she didn't know how mad Sam was with her.

"I never told you why I became an EMT, did I?"

That was the moment Chrissie realized that for all the time they'd spent together between the ambulance and the field, they really didn't know all that much about each other. "No."

"I was driving back from dinner with my mom. We were celebrating a case that I closed. It was early January, and there was black ice on the road..." Sam broke off with a shaky sigh. "I don't remember much, but I woke up upside down in an embankment. They had to cut me out of the car."

Chrissie didn't have to ask what had happened to her mother. She could tell by that thousand-yard stare—she'd seen it enough times in the families of patients to recognize it anywhere. "I'm so sorry."

"It's why I quit my job at the firm," she explained, her voice hollow and lifeless, and so unlike the voice Chrissie was used to. "I saw what those EMT's did for me, what they tried to do for my mom, and I realized I wanted to do that. I wanted to help."

She laughed tearfully, shaking her head slowly. "Some help I've been. I'm pathetic."

"Don't say that."

"I am," she whispered, finally meeting Chrissie's gaze properly, for the first time in weeks. "Look what happened back at the crash. I can't work like this; I can't risk patient's lives like that."

"You aren't pathetic, Sam," Chrissie assured her. "When I look at you, that's not what I see."

"It's not?"

The urge to grab her hand was back again, and this time Chrissie didn't fight it. She laced her fingers with Sam's, giving them a gentle squeeze. "You're the furthest thing from pathetic I've ever seen."

Sam looked at her for a few seconds, almost like she was trying to decide something. Finally, she moved forward, closing the gap between them on the couch. She paused just inches from Chrissie, so close that their breath mingled in front of their faces. Chrissie realized the younger woman was giving her an opportunity to back out, to get up and walk away before things went further.

She didn't take it.

Instead, she leaned into the kiss, pressing her lips to Sam's gently. This kiss was nothing like the first one. There was none of that frustration, none of that anger that had driven them the first time. Instead, it was sweet, almost tender.

Sam was the one to break apart as Chrissie's hands drifted to her hips to pull her closer. She didn't pull back far, just enough to speak. "Bedroom?"

Chrissie just nodded in agreement—she didn't trust herself to speak. Sam took her hand and led her through the small apartment, into the bedroom. The curtains were still drawn, so the room was only weakly lit by whatever sunlight could filter through the cloth.

Even in that pale lighting, Chrissie was struck by just how beautiful Sam was. It was something she'd always known, but she'd buried it underneath all the things about Sam that drove her crazy—she was a pain in the ass, or stubborn, or entitled.

But she was also beautiful.

Chrissie kissed her again, slowly this time, like she was trying to savor every last second. Her hands reached up to cradle Sam's face, her touch so light it was like she was afraid she'd break. It was such a world away from the first time, where the kisses had burned their lips, and their touches left bruises, and both of them knew it.

Chapter 12

With each button, she became a little more undone. Mesmerized by need and the fascination of Chrissie's long fingers. How quickly and expertly they moved. The dexterity and ease with which they worked.

As her shirt fell open, the warmth of hands against the lace of her bra electrified her body, her nipples hardening in approval. The twinge she felt in her core as her nipple was gently tweaked evoked a gasp, and it took a second for her to register the sound as her own.

The shirt slipped from her shoulders, falling at her feet. Small kisses worked their way along her collarbone. She grasped handfuls of Chrissie's hair, throwing her own head back in delight.

She wanted Chrissie more than she dared admit. Every touch of her fingers against Sam's skin magnified her need tenfold, but she knew Chrissie was teasing this encounter out. Savoring every moment. The kisses moved down to the tops of her breasts, causing her own breathing to rasp. With a quick unclip of the back of her bra, she felt the cool air on her nipples followed by the soft warmth of Chrissie's mouth and flicks of her tongue. The pleasure was excruciating.

Her belt was unfastened with as much ease, and her cargo pants slipped down and away. As she kicked off her remaining clothes, Chrissie, too, had torn off her clothes. Sam couldn't help but marvel at the firmness of her body. The slender lines she knew she would kiss her way down later. The air was tense as they brought their bodies back together again, sharing a tender kiss. .

Sam pulled away, moving to the bed. She slid her way slowly up the bed, never taking her eyes off Chrissie.

"I need you to come here." A small smile tugged at the corners of her mouth nervously. Sam watched and for the first time Chrissie seemed unsure of herself, hesitating before kneeling between Sam's legs, then lowering herself down to kiss her.

"I want to kiss every inch of your body." The first kiss started on her jawline, then down to her throat. Chrissie's warm breath on her neck made her body tingle. From her collarbone, down over her breasts, then her stomach before glancing across her hips and down the curve of her legs, Sam felt Chrissie's soft lips against her skin.

"Please." Sam's eyes, wide with desperation, met Chrissie's, and neither moved for a second. "Chrissie, I need you. Please."

She felt Chrissie's hands curl under her butt, lifting her up and parting her legs. Her head fell back with hands covering her eyes as her breathing came in short, grating breaths. Excruciating excitement swept over her as the heat of Chrissie's tongue toyed with her clit before delving deep into her. She gave herself over to the waves of pleasure that came with every lick, with the ever changing tempo. Every time she felt her orgasm build, Chrissie changed her rhythm and focus, teasing Sam until she was losing control.

With a last gasp, she reached out and held Chrissie's shoulder. "Wait. I want you to… " Her cheeks flushed with embarrassment as she looked down and met Chrissie's eyes.

"Tell me what you want, Sam, please?"

Sam's sigh was audible. "There's a… " She paused again, her cheeks burning. Shaking her head she looked into Chrissie's expectant face, her eyebrows raised in question. "There's a strap-on in the drawer at the side. I don't know if… " She shrugged before letting her head fall back, silently cursing herself for even asking.

"Oh, I think I can accommodate that." Chrissie teasingly ran her fingers up Sam's inner thigh as she moved to open the drawer at the side of the bed. She pulled out the strap-on and harness, giving Sam a quick wink as she did so. Pulling the soft plastic straps apart so she could step into it, she tightened it into position, allowing it to pull gently at the side of her clit. Taking the small tube of lube from the drawer, she flipped open the lid, squeezing a small amount onto her fingers before rubbing it over the length of the bright blue shaft. Sam ran her finger along her bottom lip, sucking gently on its tip as she watched Chrissie. Her legs widened in expectation as Chrissie turned, standing proud.

"I want you to sit on my lap." She shuffled Sam across the bed slightly so she could sit on the bed, propped on the pillows behind her. "Come here."

Sam knelt above Chrissie's lap, biting her bottom lip as the older woman massaged lube across her already wet center. She closed her eyes, losing herself in the sensation of the older woman's teasing fingers. Chrissie's hands moved to her hips, pulling her down slightly until the tip of the dildo took over the teasing.

"I want to see you come." Chrissie's words caused Sam's eyes to widen.

Sam felt Chrissie's hand on the small of her back, guiding

her towards the tip which was now teasing her entrance. She lowered herself down with a gentle moan, placing her arms around Chrissie's shoulders, looking directly at her. Slowly lifting and lowering, she began to move with Chrissie, enjoying how deeply she was being fucked.

"You are so beautiful." The words rang in Sam's ears as she felt Chrissie's hands pull her hips down deeper with every grind. As the tempo increased so did the volume and intensity of her rapture until finally she gave into her orgasm, releasing her pleasure. This time it was Chrissie's turn to gasp.

They clung to each other, the sweat from their bodies mingling, bound in the moment.

Chapter 13

"So, what now?"

Sam's voice was quiet, almost like she was afraid of the answer. They were curled up together in Sam's bed, fingertips tracing light patterns on naked skin, slowly coming down from the high.

Chrissie's fingers stilled against her skin where she'd been drawing a figure of eights, and she thought about it for a few seconds. All the reasons for them *not* to keep ending up like this were still there. There was still the age gap, they still drove each other crazy.

But there was something else, something about Sam that was addictive. The past three weeks had been hell on earth, and Chrissie realized at that moment that she never wanted to go through that again. She never wanted Sam to act like she wasn't there, like she couldn't hear or see her.

So when she kissed the blonde gently, a smile on her lips, Chrissie knew that her answer would be different this time. She knew this conversation wouldn't end in a fight.

"I want to take you to dinner," Chrissie whispered,

stroking strands of blonde hair back from Sam's face. "Somewhere nice."

"Like a date?" she asked expectantly. Chrissie laughed, nodding happily.

"Yeah, a date. You like Italian food?"

"There are people who *don't* like Italian food?"

"Fair point." Chrissie smiled warmly, trying to ignore the way her heart sped up when Sam curled up to her, nestling her head in the crook of her shoulder.

"What's everyone going to say?"

Chrissie thought about that for a moment, remembering Terri's earlier words. Finally, what she'd said back on the field made sense. *Actually, I think I've only seen you fight like this with one other person before.* Charlotte. She was talking about Charlotte.

She smiled gently, reaching down to lace her fingers with Sam's. "You know what? I think they might already know."

"You do?"

"Mmh." She squeezed Sam's hand gently, and they fell into a comfortable silence for a few seconds.

"M'tired," Sam finally mumbled, her voice muffled into Chrissie's shoulder.

"Get some sleep, Sam."

"Will you be here when I wake up?"

"Of course, I will," she promised, smiling gently. "I'm not going anywhere."

It had been a week, and for the most part Sam and Chrissie had managed to keep their blossoming relationship secret. At work they rarely saw other EMTs, so it was fairly easy. Practice was another matter entirely.

The rest of the team was shocked to arrive at practice and find Sam already there, dressed in her kit. Even more surprising, she and Chrissie were talking together, giggling over some inside joke. To most of the team, it just seemed like they'd finally broken through whatever was driving them so crazy and were starting to see eye to eye.

For Terri, though, it was glaringly obvious what had happened. She picked up on the way they leaned into each other when they spoke, subconsciously trying to close any distance that separated them. She caught the stolen glances they thought no one else saw; she spotted those hidden, secretive smiles. It didn't take long for the pieces to fall together, and for her to realize what was going on.

She hung around after practice, deliberately taking her time as she got out of her kit. She folded her clothes very deliberately, glancing at Sam out of the corner of her eye to see the young blonde doing the same thing. Around them, the rest of the team filtered out one by one, until finally they were the last two.

It didn't take long for Chrissie to arrive after the team left. She stopped short when she realized Terri was still in the locker room, waiting patiently with a knowing smile on her face.

"I thought you'd left."

Terri shrugged, adjusting the strap of her backpack. "Figured I'd wait and get you two alone."

Sam and Chrissie exchanged uncertain glances. They hadn't planned on telling anyone for a few weeks—they just wanted to spend some time getting to know each other, settling into this new relationship before they went public with the news.

Terri grinned, patting Chrissie on the shoulder as she

passed by her to the door. She leaned in close, whispering her final verdict.

"Called it."

Chrissie laughed at that, relief flooding over her like a wave. Of course that was all Terri was concerned about—being right. Her friend paused at the door, turning to look at the room for a few seconds. She met Chrissie's gaze and smiled warmly.

"You two look good together."

Chrissie felt heat rush to her cheeks at that, and she couldn't help the smile that broke out across her face. "Thanks."

"We should go for a drink sometime." She pointed over at Sam. "I like you, O'Shea. But I still have to vet you."

"Understood." Sam laughed, walking over to stand beside Chrissie. For a few seconds none of them spoke. There was nothing more that needed to be said, especially not when Chrissie laced her fingers into Sam's. That said everything they couldn't find the words for.

"See you two at work." Terri smiled, walking out and letting the door swing shut behind her. Her retreating footsteps got fainter and fainter as she left them, and when they were finally alone, Sam rested her head on Chrissie's shoulder, nuzzling into her. Chrissie couldn't help it when her smile stretched wider at the weight on her shoulder, and she squeezed Sam's hand gently, content to just stay there for a little while, in their own personal bubble.

Chapter 14

ONE YEAR LATER...

"I can't believe you are still going over that game plan. I'm sure you were muttering about it in your sleep last night." Sam bent her head forward, tipping her blonde hair into the towel and patting it dry. "You know we'll win. Since Gabby joined us, we're a crack team. What was it Terri called us last night? The dynamic duo!"

Sam bounced onto the bed, causing Chrissie to roll into the newly created dip. Chrissie pursed her lips and raised an eyebrow. "Well, let's see if the dynamic duo help us win the cup and then you can crow about it." She had been up since seven, showered, and changed and was now sitting in her sweats, making sure every eventuality for the game had been covered.

Sam loved how seriously Chrissie took the game, both on and off the field. She'd been playing for Allston Stars FC for three years now, but Chrissie had been with the team for almost fifteen years, playing and then coaching. This was the first time they had ever gotten within touching distance of the Women's State Cup. She'd watched Chrissie and Marta, the team's manager, spend hours together selecting the strongest team, working out their strategy and game plan. Their opponents were the Salem Sliders FC who had won the cup for the last four years in a row, mainly on account of their six-foot tall blonde striker, Lucy Aimes.

This year they had their own secret weapon, Gabby Ellis. While Gabby didn't have Lucy's height, she was fast and fearless, never shying away from a full-on tackle. Gabby took no prisoners, either on the field or in the ER where she worked as a doctor. Chrissie had moved Sam into the right wingback position, pushing her hard in training to get her speed up, and it was paying off in allowing her to create opportunities for Gabby to finish. Chrissie had been the first to see their potential chemistry on the field and placing them together had been a stroke of genius.

It wasn't the chemistry on the field that was on Sam's mind as she started stroking Chrissie's neck. Tiny, light fingertip touches that were guaranteed to drive her insane with want. "You need to blow off a little steam before the game. Release all that tension." As the small kisses landed, following her fingertips, Chrissie stretched her neck to the side, allowing Sam full access.

"I can't. Sam, you know I can never resist you when you start that." Chrissie squirmed. Sam knew Chrissie's clit would be starting to throb gently and with a simple slide of her hand beneath the waistband of her sweats, it would be game on.

"Are you sure you want to keep the no sex before a game rule?" Sam ran the very tip of her tongue up the curve of Chrissie's neck before stopping at her earlobe and whispering, "I could make it worth your while." The warmth of Sam's breath sent a visible shudder of desire through Chrissie's body but rather than capitulating, she jumped up off the bed, leaving Sam in her wake.

"No, you're not going to do this to me. Not just now. Not before the big game. You've got your therapy session to go to, and I have to get all the kit down to the club. But I'll tell you what…" Bending forward, Chrissie placed one hand on Sam's knee before sliding it up under her towel. "If we win that cup today, I'll give you everything and anything you want." Her fingers made little circles as she played with the soft, fair skin on the inside of Sam's thighs.

Sam saw the smile on Chrissie's face as her legs widened involuntarily under her touch.

"You are so damned beautiful. But first, the cup." Chrissie's tone was decisive.

Falling back onto the bed, Sam let out a huge groan. "I could leave the therapist. Just phone her and say I have a migraine. She wouldn't mind. I'm hardly ever getting nightmares now I've moved in with you and when was the last time I was late for anything?"

"If you don't put some clothes on and get your lazy ass up, you'll be late for therapy." Chrissie held out a hand to pull Sam to her feet. It was grudgingly grasped and as they came level, Sam allowed her body to be pulled in tight to Chrissie's side. "You are doing great, and I am so proud of you but don't stop now. You are doing too well." Chrissie's lips were soft and welcoming, pulling Sam deeply into the kiss.

"Okay, I'll go. But I'm holding you to 'everything and anything' when we win today!" Sam's smile was wicked and loaded with the promise of taking all she wanted and possibly a bit more. *If only you knew all the things I want to do to you.*

"When we win. I like it, that's the positive mental attitude we need!" Chrissie gathered her papers together and, raising her head, she saw Sam's towel drop from her body and crumple on the floor. Sam knew her resolve wanted to go the same way.

"Everything and anything..." Sam said the words whilst running her hands over the length of her body, getting a huge kick as Chrissie's eyes widened.

Chapter 15

The chatter was building as nerves began to take hold in the dressing room. Bags and clothes were strewn over the benches and banter was being thrown about in good humor. Most of the team were dressed and Terri, who was normally bright and lively, was a little quieter as she tied her boots.

"Terri, you're not saying much. Are you feeling okay?" Sam didn't want to draw too much attention, so her words were said in a low tone as she sat down next to her.

"Yeh. I just can't believe we've made it to the cup, you know?" She shrugged, raising her palms in an open, questioning gesture. "I never thought I'd see the day and I know how much this means to Chrissie and Marta. Fuck, how much this means to us all." She shook her head slightly.

"Hey, don't get nervous. No matter what happens, it's just a game, right? You can only do what you can do." Sam knew how overwhelming the whole thing was, even though she tried to make her words sound as reassuring as possible.

"Right, listen up, ladies." The shout was accompanied by a waft of cold air as Chrissie and Marta made their entrance.

Chrissie laid out the play sheets onto the large wide bench in the middle of the room. As Sam looked at the notes and diagrams spread out wide across the wooden surface, she had a flashback of laying Chrissie down there for the first time. A flush rose up from Sam's chest, reaching her cheeks. Catching herself lost in reliving that moment, she had a quick sneaky glance around, almost checking no one else could see the pictures which were in her mind.

"Here is how today is going to play out." Chrissie glanced up, making sure she had everyone's attention. Marta leant her tall, angular frame against the lockers with her arms crossed over her chest and nodded for Chrissie to continue. "We're going to be playing a five-four-one formation. These Salem girls have a vicious attack, so we need our defense to be as strong as possible. Make no mistake though, we are not going to be letting them control the tempo of this game. We want to be creating as many opportunities upfront as we can. It is all about getting that ball forward and in the right half of the field."

By the time Chrissie was finished, the girls were fired up. Looks of determination flashed between them. They were focused. They were ready. "Shut Up and Dance With Me" blasted through the changing room. With adrenaline pumping so hard, you could almost taste the anticipation. This was their time, and nothing was going to stop them.

"Are we ready?" Chrissie's voice boomed through the room.

"Hell, yes!" was the united returning scream.

"Right, let's go get what's ours!"

Marta held the door to the changing room open. With the scream of warriors, Sam, their captain, led them out to battle. There was no stopping them now.

Salem won the toss and they took early possession, but Allston kept their heads up and Sam made sure of that. They pressed hard, forcing Salem back to their end of the field at every opportunity. The pace was fast, and Sam could feel the burn in her legs as she ran with the ball up the outside of the field, dodging the opposition's midfielders with quick directional changes.

The back four of Salem were all over Sam and Gabby, aiming to cut them off at every opportunity. Twice Gabby had taken a long shot at goal, only for it to hit the post and deflect off. Sam had placed the corners perfectly in the center of the eighteen-yard box, and Gabby had come so close once with a header, then again with an acrobatic back kick that got her cheers from the thousand or so supporters that had come along to watch.

As the half-time whistle blew, it was nil-nil, and neither side was ready to concede defeat.

"Fuck me, they are playing hard." Gabby ran alongside Sam as they left the field, running back towards the changing rooms. Catching sight of Tara and Phelps standing together, she waved her arm straight up in the air to catch their attention. Four arms waved back at her with mad vigor. The air was filled with chatter and swearing at some of the referee's more questionable decisions as the girls replenished their fluids for the second half.

A hush filled the room when Chrissie and Marta came in. The women knew they would have loved them to have taken the advantage by now. Lord knows they had been given enough opportunities. Sam watched as Gabby's head dipped down, her eyes focused on the floor. Sam suddenly felt defensive of her teammates. They had played hard, forced Salem to make mistakes and so what if they hadn't managed to secure points yet? They were doing their damndest to maximize the opportunities. If Chrissie wanted to have a go, she was ready.

But Chrissie didn't chew them out or yell or scream. She gathered them around, and in an even tone, she spoke. "We knew this wasn't going to be easy, and they aren't making it easy for us, but you are forcing their hand at every opportunity, grabbing every chance when they slip up. I am proud of you all, but we aren't there yet. This is ours for the taking. I can smell it, it's so close. So far we've been playing with them." Chrissie paused, bringing herself up to full height. "But now we start working." There were a few *yeh's* and some hard swallows around the room. Each of the women made eye contact and offered small nods. They were one.

With growing volume and tempo, Chrissie sent the message home to each and every one of them. "I believe in you. Your manager believes in you, and your captain believes in you. This is your time to shine, ladies. Fucking shine like the stars you are!" Chrissie punched the air and was greeted with a rally of voices shouting, "Hell, yeah!"

Even Marta was close to tears by the time she had finished.

With a renewed determination bursting out of their chests, they started the second half with one aim: ownership of the game. Salem were getting desperate with a few dirty tackles, but the referee saw a clear advantage to Sam and her team, and waved play on. Carla, the left wing-back, made a great lob to just outside the penalty box, and Gabby took full advantage by thumping it straight into the left-hand corner of the net. The whole place went wild and the team piled on top of Gabby, but they still had fifteen minutes to go. With everything to play for, Salem knew they had nothing left to lose and went full throttle with slamming attacks. One Salem player was red-carded and sent off and a second yellow-carded, but it didn't tone the game down.

With only five minutes left, Salem caught a lucky break, converting a questionable penalty and bringing the game to a tie. The shouting between Allston gained volume, cheering each other to keep their heads up. And then it happened. Sam received the ball, and with an opening ahead of her, she took the opportunity and charged down the right-hand side of the field. Gabby anticipated Sam's play and seized the moment, sidestepping the defense to place herself in the perfect position for maximizing the cross as it left Sam's boot. The next few seconds seemed to happen in slow motion. As Salem's goalkeeper launched herself in anticipation to the left, Gabby's header sent the ball to the right, punching waves through the net and securing them the lead.

As they hugged each other in elation, Chrissie waved her arms, desperately trying to get them to retain their focus for the final few minutes of the match. With grins bursting from ear to ear, they kept the pressure on Salem, watching their opponent's shoulders fall in defeat as the final whistle was blown.

The cheers and hollers from the crowd filled their ears, and Gabby and Sam were lifted precariously and unceremoniously onto their teammate's shoulders for about thirty seconds before being tumbled back down to earth.

The award ceremony was short and sweet with the mayor milking the photo opportunity for the promotion of women's sport in the city, but no one cared because they had won the cup for the first time in the club's history. Tara, Phelps, and even Steve O'Reilly, who'd made a last-minute appearance to support his EMT crew, made an impromptu field invasion with hugs and cheers. They sent the women off to get changed with orders to meet at the bar at the end of the road as soon as they were showered and dressed. Champagne corks popped in the changing rooms in celebration, and every player toasted their team's success many times over. It was a moment none of them would ever forget.

Chapter 16

As the last of the women left with high spirits and headed off to celebrate, only Chrissie and Sam remained. Leaning with her back against the door, Chrissie watched her girlfriend pull her shirt over her defined, albeit slightly bruised, muscles.

"You did good today. Really good, and I couldn't be prouder of you."

"Yeh, well I had a fairly good incentive, and I don't mean the cup, although it is very nice." Sam nodded to the cup, which sat on their bench. "When a woman says you can have —what was it now? Everything? Anything? Then it tends to focus your mind."

Chrissie kept eye contact with Sam as she closed the gap between them.

"It was such a waste getting showered. I much prefer it when you are nice and sweaty." Chrissie's hands slid around Sam's waist, pulling her close. "And when I said you could have everything and anything, I meant it. Anything you want. But first we have gotta take the cup to the bar and celebrate. Everyone's waiting for us."

"You can't be serious? I could have you here, right now, screaming my name and you'd rather have a Bud?" Sam was incredulous but smiling. Nothing could tarnish this day. "Is this your way of telling me the romance has gone?" she joked.

"You tell me in about eight hours if the romance has gone. Sometimes the best things in life are worth waiting for." She leant in as she spoke and slipped her hand around the back of Sam's head, pulling her in for a long, lingering kiss. As Sam's mouth opened in anticipation, Chrissie flicked her tongue in slowly, teasing her. Within seconds, the kiss had deepened, and Chrissie slid her hand down inside Sam's jeans.

"You really are ready for this, aren't you?" A wicked grin spread over her lips. "I could take you now but I want to tease you for a bit longer." Chrissie's fingers gently slid down further, twisting into her wetness before pulling out slightly to run back and forth on either side of her clit. A low moan escaped from Sam's mouth. "I am going to tease you and flirt with you all night, and then you get to call the shots. That is your reward for being my player of the match." With a final rougher pull over her clit she pulled out of Sam's jeans, leaving her with a look of palpable need and desolation.

"You can't leave me like this."

"Grab your bag. Come on, everyone is waiting." Chrissie grabbed the cup from the bench and turned to make for the door, giving Sam a quick wink.

"You bitch. I'm going to make you pay for this later." Grabbing her bag, she chased after Chrissie as they both ran out the door.

A cheer erupted as they walked into the bar. Gabby was standing on the seating at the back of the large booth they had claimed as their own, trying desperately to release the cork from yet another bottle of champagne.

"We thought you were never coming!" Tara shouted before ducking down fast as the cork flew past her ear with a loud bang. "Jesus Gabby, that's another three years of my life I'll never get back!"

"Pass these over! Chrissie, Sam, you haven't got a glass yet. Grab these." Tara, Gabby's girlfriend, was playing mom and filling champagne flutes, trying to make sure everyone had a drink.

The *ting, ting, ting* of metal on glass brought a little hush to the room, and everyone's attention turned to Marta. "Can I have your attention?" With murmurings and low level chatting still continuing, Marta tried again. "Everyone, can I get some quiet, please? Thank you. I just want to raise a toast to the incredible Allston Stars… To the best bunch of women I have ever had the pleasure of working and playing with. And I've played with more than a few of you over the years!"

A cheer of "Oy, Oy!" rang out from the back of the crowd.

"It's always nice to get a bit of additional support from the players in the room at times like this! But seriously I am so damned proud of every one one of you!"

The place erupted into cheers, and then Terri stood, readying the crowd yet again with a further *ting, ting, ting*. "On behalf of all the *players*—" She tipped a wink at Marta before continuing. "I'd just like to say a huge thank you to Marta and Chrissie who have led us to victory. We couldn't have done it without you! And of course we all know that it is really the EMTs who are the driving force behind the team's victory! Go the EMTs!"

An explosion of cheers and boos burst out around them,

with every City General department claiming to have the best players and teasing each other with friendly banter.

Chrissie sat down next to Tara, laughing at the surrounding mayhem. "It's nice to see you here supporting Gabby. She played really well today. You make a good couple."

"You think?" Tara raised an eyebrow, her smile broad.

"I think." Chrissie nodded as if evaluating the pairing. "You bring out the best in each other, and that's what it's all about. I haven't seen you this happy in years, not since—well, I was going to say Bob, but you were never that happy with Bob, understandably."

Tara nodded. "That was a long time dead before it finished. I suppose I just didn't realize how much of life I was missing out on while I was with him. Gabby is everything Bob wasn't. She is passionate, outgoing, fun, honest..."

"A woman."

"Yes, a woman." Tara felt a blush rise over her cheeks.

"I'm only teasing. It's good having you join us on the dark side." Chrissie let out a chuckle.

"What's so funny?"

"I'm trying to imagine just how bent out of shape Bob must have been about you and Gabby." A small snort escaped. "Sorry. I shouldn't laugh, but I know he can't have taken that well." Chrissie knew she might be overstepping the mark but after a couple of glasses of champagne, her boundaries had been lowered. Tara's smile reassured her she hadn't gone too far.

"Don't apologize. No, he didn't take it well." This time it was Tara's turn to laugh as she remembered the scene in his office where he tried to recover his dented pride. "I think I dented his manhood. He was so shocked he even backed off slashing the community project budget, which had to be the best silver lining I could have asked for. Not backed off completely, but at least he has given us the opportunity to keep much of the budget while we fundraise for the rest." Tara shrugged her shoulders, laughing.

"And how is that going? The fundraising, I mean." Chrissie had to raise her voice as Gabby and Sam were still battling over which area would win at a five-a-side football match. The fun teasing had reached fever pitch between them with arms gesticulating wildly. It was a sight that filled Chrissie up with a warm glow. So much energy and enthusiasm all wrapped up into one woman. Her attention was averted by Tara.

"Slow. Most of it is dry and boring gala dinners. It'd be nice to have something a bit more fun. It's nice to have things with a bit more life about them." She laughed, nodding towards Sam and Gabby.

Chrissie nodded as if understanding, but the reality was she had never been to one of the hospital's gala events, nor had she any yearning to attend. It was all a bit stuffy for her. She'd much rather share beer, pizza and a Netflix box set with Sam any day of the week. She let her eyes wander around the crowd in front of them. The vast majority of women on the team, and those who had come to support them, worked in one area or another of the hospital. They all loved soccer and the camaraderie it brought. And then an idea struck her.

Turning fully to face Tara, she let the rapidly forming thoughts tumble out of her mouth. "I've got an idea. Now, this might be crazy but hear me out. What if we had a City General five-a-side charity playoff? One or two teams from every department? So the ER could have one and obviously the EMTs would have a team. Cardio, Oncology, hell we could even get Melanie's ass in a pair of shorts and get the admin team involved."

The idea of Melanie running around a field in salmon

pink linen shorts, screaming every time the ball came near her, had the two of them in kinks of laughter.

"Just think about it. Teams could pay to be submitted, and every team could raise money through sponsorship. It would be a great awareness thing, and we could get the community engaged too. What do you think? Does it sound crazy?"

Tara seemed to be mulling the idea over, and she sat nodding. "It doesn't sound the least bit crazy. It sounds like a great idea. That could be so much fun. But it would take a hell of a lot of organizing. Wouldn't it? I don't think we'd have a problem getting teams to sign up. In fact, I could see people arguing over securing a space on the team."

"What if I said leave the organizing of the games to me and we'll get a few others to help with getting the teams together, and get some publicity? Would you be up for it?"

Tara mused for a moment and then gave a decisive nod. "Hell, yeh!"

Chapter 17

The enthusiasm for the idea had taken hold of the whole group as their celebrations continued into the evening with half the teams being suggested or picked out already. There were no rules on how the teams were made up; there just needed to be five on each side. Chrissie knew the idea was gold, and seeing Sam's enthusiasm for it on top of winning the cup made her heart so happy. As the first few people started to head off home to their families, Chrissie had caught Sam's eye, mouthing the words "everything and anything."

It had taken Sam seconds to down the rest of her drink and grab her jacket, declaring to everyone around her "she'd pulled!" before leading Chrissie by the hand to the waiting Uber.

Dropping their bags where they landed behind the closed door, Sam pulled Chrissie into her embrace. Their lips sought out the other, and the playful kisses very quickly deepened into something far more urgent. Sam wanted to feel the touch of Chrissie's bare skin, slipping her hands under her shirt and gently letting her short nails scratch down her back. The resulting moan from Chrissie ignited a slow, wicked smile across Sam's face.

"Everything and anything? Right?" Her eyebrows were raised in question as she pulled her head back to take in Chrissie's response.

"Whatever you want." Chrissie's voice hitched. Sam wasn't sure if it was nervousness or anticipation, but she sure as shit was going to make tonight memorable. Taking Chrissie's hand, she led her through to their bedroom before pulling her in again and placing teasing kisses on her lips, her neck, and down to her collarbone. Taking her time, she methodically removed every item of clothing Chrissie wore, slowly kissing and touching every area of exposed flesh they revealed. It was one long, never-ending tease.

When Chrissie was completely naked, Sam pushed her back onto the bed, pushing her back up to the very top with motivational kisses. "You know how we talked about experimenting just a little and taking it up a notch? Well, seeing as we won today, I'm thinking this might be the perfect time."

Sam was aware of Chrissie's eyes widening as she removed each item of clothing. The fact the woman she loved was lying back, touching herself in anticipation of what Sam had planned for her made her heart race. The look of desire on Chrissie's face was mingled with curiosity as Sam opened the dresser drawer, pulling out a few long, soft scarves.

Climbing onto the bed, Sam made her way up to straddle Chrissie's body. Her excitement brushed against the older woman's torso, and the smile and moans of appreciation didn't fall on deaf ears. Kissing her gently, Sam then whispered, "Put your hands above your head for me?" She noted Chrissie's slight hesitation. "I promise, I'll only give you pleasure and if you feel uncomfortable at all, just say. If you don't want to, we don't have to." Sam held still, awaiting Chrissie's response.

"I want to. God, I thought it was obvious I want to." She nodded down to the gleaming wetness between her legs.

"Okay, a safe word then? What about 'I love Trump' because nothing will stop me faster than hearing you say those words?" Their laughter filled the room.

"If I can get these words out, then we know we are in trouble. But yeh, oddly, that works for me." With a nod, Sam was given permission to loosely tie one end of the scarves around her wrists and the other to the bedposts. Sam took in Chrissie's body, arms spread out wide above her head. Sam held the third scarf, running the soft fabric between her hands, nudging her knee tighter into Chrissie's center. The warm wetness coated her skin. Sam could smell it in the air, and she licked her lips in anticipation of the taste.

"They say removing more of your senses heightens the pleasure. I could blindfold you too?" She wanted to give Chrissie the best orgasm of her life but equally, this was new territory for them as a couple, and she wanted this to be good, clean fun.

"I'm game. Everything and anything." Chrissie winked and blew Sam a kiss, a sight which sent an electric twinge straight to Sam's clit. Fuck, she loved how hot this woman was. Fuck, she loved her.

With the final scarf in place, Sam pressed her weight onto Chrissie. There was an electric touch as their bare skin met.

"I'm going to take this long and slow. I could be here for hours." Sam's promise was met with a moan as Chrissie pushed her head back into the pillow, exposing her neck. Sam's lips connected with the soft flesh, kissing and licking. Featherlight kisses to her neck and collarbone were followed by little nips and tiny sucks as she made her way down her chest. At all times, she kept the weight of her body pressed hard against Chrissie's wet, pulsing core. Their breathing was shallow. Rasping.

As Sam sucked on Chrissie's nipple, she felt her body shudder with pleasure underneath her. A harder suck followed by the tiniest tug and Chrissie's back was arching, allowing her to press hard against Sam's body.

Sam's laugh was light. "How much are you enjoying this?" Her hands running with the lightest touch over Chrissie's body were so obviously driving her wild.

"You're cruel. The best type of cruel, but cruel." A shudder rippled through Chrissie's body, causing her words to reverberate as they hit the hot air of the room.

Sliding down further, kissing over her stomach, Sam eventually slid her face over Chrissie's short trimmed hair. The tickle of the roughness gave way to the yielding soft folds of excitement as she allowed herself to savor the full taste of the woman she loved.

"Oh christ, Sam!" Chrissie's pleading filled the room, her body writhing up desperately, seeking out more and more of Sam's mouth and flattened tongue. Sam felt Chrissie's hips buck hard against her face, the desperation in the speed and fury of the movements. "Fuck me, please. Fuck me hard. Harder than you've ever done."

Teasing fingers promised, then lingered, driving Chrissie closer and closer to the edge. Then stopped.

"Turn over for me and raise your ass in the air? Please?" Sam had the feeling whatever wish she requested in that moment would have been granted, but she waited for a response.

"What—shit. Yes, okay."

Sam had tied the scarves with enough length they could be twisted, allowing Chrissie's arms to cross as she turned over onto her knees with her body pulled forward. Placing both hands on Chrissie's hips, Sam had a surge of excitement as her bare ass proudly raised in front of her. Sliding her tongue down from the base of her back, Sam held nothing back in her exploration, stopping only to allow herself the smallest of smiles as Chrissie released the lowest guttural moan she'd ever heard. Sliding and curling her fingers deep inside Chrissie's warm wet want, Sam thought her heart was about to explode out of her chest. The desire, the love, the primal need between them in that moment was overwhelming; they both gave themselves in their entirety. Pulling almost out and then deep in again, harder and faster with every thrust, Sam felt her fingers being squeezed tighter and tighter. The groans from Chrissie were becoming louder to almost a scream.

"Don't stop. Just don't fucking stop."

"Stop? I'm going to fuck you like this until you can't walk any longer." Sam's promise was the final tipping point and Chrissie came hard, fast, and wet over Sam's hand. A smile burst across her face, stretching from ear to ear, and while she slowed her movements down to a gentle rhythm, she didn't stop. Sam merely allowed Chrissie to catch her breath before increasing once more to build the second, then the third wave of pleasure.

They were both panting hard, sweat dripping from their bodies when Chrissie eventually said, "Enough. Enough. I can't take it anymore. Please don't make me say those words."

Sam wiggled her fingers in a light butterfly movement, sending a series of twitches through Chrissie's body. "I've never had this much control over a woman." Her giggle was light and playful. "I could be really cruel, just to hear you say them." The movement of one finger was enough to make Chrissie plead for mercy.

"If you love me, you won't!"

Her pleas were heard as Sam gently withdrew, folding

herself over the top of Chrissie's raised ass, wrapping her arms around her middle.

"I'll never stop loving you." She squeezed gently before helping Chrissie ease onto her side and sliding her wrists free of the soft fabric.

Facing each other, noses touching, Chrissie's voice was gentle. "I have no idea what I did to deserve you, but I don't want this to ever change. This—we—are perfect." She tilted her head, placing a tiny kiss on the end of Sam's nose. "I couldn't love you any more than I do now."

Sam closed her eyes, smiling. *What a fucking amazing day.* It was the tickle of fabric on the inside of her wrist and the sudden movement of the mattress that roused her back into full consciousness again.

"What? You think I'm letting you off that easy?" Chrissie's long fingers had the scarves in place in seconds. "You're up for this, right?"

Sam could only laugh at Chrissie's enthusiasm. "I think you might enjoy this a bit too much!" She shuffled herself across the middle of the bed. "What are you doing with the last scarf?"

"Well, I was going to blindfold you too, but I'm thinking maybe a gag!" Chrissie doubled over in giggles at the alarm on Sam's face. "Like anyone could ever shut you up." Reaching over to the bedside dresser Chrissie pulled out *the* drawer. "No blindfold for you. I want you to see what's coming." Chrissie's raised eyebrow and devilish smirk made Sam swallow hard in excitement. Nothing was being held back tonight.

Independent authors like me are completely dependent on reviews. The truth is simple:

Good reviews = Amazon recommending this book = my ability to write more stories.

You don't even need to write words—just leaving a quick ★★★★★ rating is enough to make a huge difference.

☞ **Leave your review here:**
   1. **AMAZON REVIEWS**
   2. **<u>APPLE REVIEWS</u>**
   2. **GOODREADS REVIEWS**
   3. **RUBYSCOTT.SHOP REVIEWS**

Thank you from Chrissie, Sam and Ruby!

Want to stay updated?

If you enjoyed this story and you'd like to know when the next one arrives, I'd love to stay in touch. My newsletter is where I share new releases, behind the scenes glimpses and exclusive extras.

No spam. You can unsubscribe at any time.

Subscribe to my Newsletter

Visit Rubyscott.shop

Ready for more?
Open Heart is waiting for you.

Also by Ruby Scott

Awakening of Desires

May I Call You Mistress?

Darkness Of Desire

Mistress of Desire

Commitment to Desire

Desire's Truth

Surrender to Desire

The Art of Deception Series

The Turning

The Reckoning

The Healing Heart Series

Rescuing Hearts

Curious Hearts

Wild Hearts

Exposed Hearts

City General: Medic 1 Series

Hot Response

Open Heart

Love Trauma

Diagnosis Love

Trails of the Heart

Healing of the Heart

The Velvet Storm Series

<u>The Stranger Within Me</u>

<u>Strangely Familiar</u>

The Stronger You Series

<u>Inside Fighter</u>

<u>Seconds Out</u>

<u>On The Ropes</u>

Standalones

<u>Blood Marks</u>

<u>Evergreen</u>

<u>No Way Out</u>

Reel vs Real

Also me, in disguise: Frankie Duncan

<u>First Comes Love</u>

<u>Love in Action</u>

<u>Her Christmas Escape</u>

And writing crime as Susie Fleming

Blood Ties

Blood Oath

Acknowledgements

As an indie author, a book's success is never a solo effort. I'm incredibly lucky to work with a team of talented humans who help make these stories possible.

From Emily Kaye, who edits my English books, to Ines, Nia, and Finn, my German dream team, every one of you brings care, skill, and heart to these pages. Emma reads my chapters as they're written, offering support, reassurance, and exactly the right words whenever I need them. And then there's Angie. Translating my words, steadying my nerves, reminding me why I started when doubt creeps in. My wife. My whole damned world.

Special mention goes to my sounding board, who heroically tackles my carefree attitude towards prepositions and my acrimonious relationship with commas, making every book stronger than the last.

You all allow me to bring these stories to life and into readers' hands. Without you, there would be no books.

I love you all.

Ruby

X

About the Author

Ruby Scott lives in a hillfoot village nestled at the foot of Scotland's Ochil Hills with her wife Angie. Her characters are shameless about waking her at 3am to discuss their problems—so rude, but she indulges them nonetheless. She frequently texts character dialogue at inappropriate moments, much to the confusion of Angie who gets them by mistake, often leaving her thinking her wife has lost her mind.

When not hosting nocturnal therapy sessions, she finds inspiration walking in nature or by the sea, where her soul calms and her heart and head fill with stories of incredible women falling in love who are always good, even when they're gloriously messy.

When not in her native Scotland, Ruby loves travelling with Angie, discovering that every encounter—whether it's similarities that create bonds or differences that teach them something new—reminds them that really, what's the point of every day if it isn't to learn? Either way, there'll be adventure.

facebook.com/RubyScottLesbianRomanceBooks
instagram.com/rubyscott_author
tiktok.com/@rubyscott.author
bookbub.com/authors/ruby-scott
threads.com/@rubyscott_author
pinterest.com/RubyScottBooks

Ruby Scott

www.rubyscott.com